T0193574

Satchmo

Written & illustrated by
Trudy L. Himes

This book belongs to:

_____

To order additional copies of this book, contact:
Xlibris
844-714-8691
www.Xlibris.com
Orders@Xlibris.com

Book Designer: Jerome Cuyos

ISBN: Softcover   978-1-5992-6619-0
        Hardcover   978-1-5992-6620-6

Library of Congress Control Number: 2005908006

Print information available on the last page

Rev. date: 01/11/2023

Satchmo

Written & illustrated
by
Trudy L. Himes

Satchmo

Satchmo is his formal name
but Mo will bring him home,
Unless he's in the hunting game
and far away did roam.

Hunting is his spice in life.
To Mo there's no exception.
Frogs and Snakes and mice and moles
are hunted with purrfection.

Fancy Dancing is his trade.
He jumps upon a rail,
Then struts along in arrogance
as he waves his lengthy tail.

He snubs the food inside his dish
and buries what he's able.
Atop the fridge he croons to me
to pull the proper label.

Winter weather brings him in
to curl upon the heat.
Underneath my table skirt
he's ever so discreet!

He's long and lean with eyes of green
and fur to match a sable.
His attitude precludes all rules
and he lounges on my table!

t. l. himes

Official
Hunting License
of the
Feline Mousiation
issued to
Satchmo
"MO"
Himes

tlhimes

Satchmo is his formal name

But "Mo" will bring him home,

Unless he's in the hunting game

And far away did roam.

Hunting is his spice in life

To Mo there's no exception.

Frogs and snakes and mice and moles

Are hunted with purrfection.

Fancy dancing is his trade.

He jumps upon a rail,

Then struts along in arrogance

As he waves his lengthy tail.

He snubs the food inside his dish

And buries what he's able.

Atop the fridge he croons to me

To pull the proper label!

Winter weather brings him in

To curl upon the heat.

Underneath my table skirt

He's ever so discreet

He's long and lean with eyes of green

and fur to match a sable.

His attitude precludes all rules

And he lounges on my table !

The End

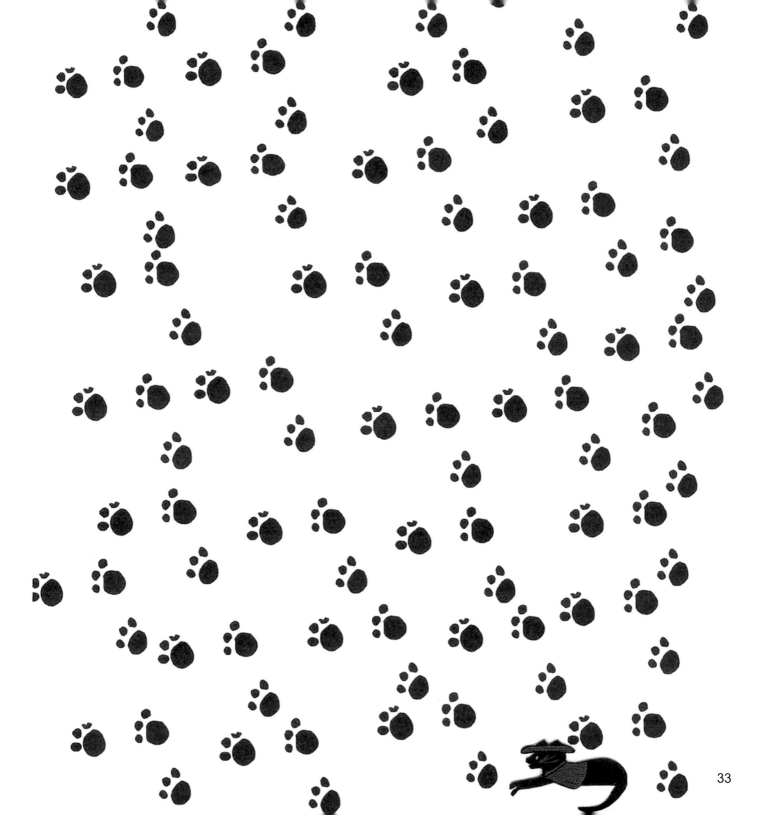

33

Printed in the United States
by Baker & Taylor Publisher Services